MOTHER

OF THE

SEA

ZETTA ELLIOTT

MOTHER
OF THE
SEA

ZETTA ELLIOTT

Rosetta
&
Press

When the skinless men leave, the taste of salt lingers on her lips. Relieved, the girl bows her head and once more kisses the tear-stained face of the child burrowing into her neck. They are both trying to hide from this nightmare. They both do what they can to disappear.

The girl clutches the child to her chest, grateful that the small body in her arms hides both her nakedness and her true age. Back in her village, she had been proud of her blossoming breasts and knew that many admiring eyes watched her hips sway as she walked home from the river with a jug of water balanced on her head. Then the raiders came to her village, shattering her peaceful life and promising future as wife of the chief's youngest son.

Now her body only shames her. For its weakness. For the ripeness that even weeks of grime and filth cannot conceal. It is the helplessness of this child who only sleeps or weeps that shames the skinless ones, making them avert their pale, hungry eyes and hastily reach past the girl to pluck some other whimpering victim from the crowded cell.

For three days and nights they have clung to one another, bound by this shared need for protection. The weight of the strange, silent child comforts the girl but does not fill the hole in her heart. She cannot forget the sight of her sister—almost the same age as the child she now cradles—wilting in the brutal sun as the coffle moved away and left her behind. The trader's blow had not killed her beloved sister. Unable to accept her fate, Adun had wept piteously for miles until the trader untied her, smashed in her small skull, and left her to die in the ditch. The girl had begged him for mercy, promising to carry her little sister the rest of the way, but the brute only spat in her face and raised the club above his head to silence her as well. The trader knew what she did not: that the march to the coast would take several more weeks and all would not survive. The dusty path they trod was littered with the bleached bones of countless broken bodies that had been cut loose and cast aside.

For countless days and nights the girl wondered whether it would have been better to share her sister's fate. Better to lie half-dead in a ditch and be devoured by some wild beast in the night than to wait in this dank cell, prey for the skinless men. They take the prettiest girls by torchlight and return them in the morning, still whimpering, badly bruised, and broken inside. The girl knew her turn would come but then one morning she woke to find a child nestled in her arms. New slaves were often brought to the cell but none had arrived during the night. The child had simply appeared out of thin air and the girl dared not question the gift the gods had bestowed upon her.

They belong to one another now. Whatever fate awaits them, they will face together. The girl silently vows that she will not let *this* child be left behind. Fatigue lets her whisper foolish promises in the child's ear. How can she—a mere girl—keep this child safe? Every few days the skinless ones unlock the cell's iron gate and drive half the women into the sea. At least, that's what she thinks must happen because amidst the barking of the skinless men and the shrieks of the terrified captives, the girl hears the splash of bodies dropping into water. Why they would march captives so far merely to drown them, she does not know. But the girl assures the child in her arms that she will not let go, not even as they sink like stones to the bottom of the sea.

The patter of the child's heart racing against her own lets the girl know that something is coming—something they should dread. The girl listens to the waves crashing against the shore and wonders if drowning hurts. She once saw a woman from her village who had drowned. Face down, she floated peacefully in the river until two boys waded out and pulled the body to shore. No one knew just how the woman had died— the river wasn't very deep, and was often full of children swimming while their mothers washed clothes and older girls like herself gathered water for cooking. Some in her village had whispered that the drowning was the work of the Spirit that lived in the river.

The girl longs to hear her mother's voice once more but those who survived the raid on her village were bound and taken off in different directions. Each lot of captives was sold to a different trader, and several sales occurred before the coffle reached the ominous white castle at the coast. It has been weeks since the girl heard her mother's tongue or saw a face like her own.

What she hopes for now is a peaceful death, an end to the

ache deep in her bones from marching so many miles with so little water or food and the traders' lash steadily licking at her flesh. The stinking cell is filled with so many bodies that she has no choice but to stand squeezed between strangers. Later, at sea, she will remember this swaying sensation, how the women's pleas in countless foreign tongues formed a lament that bound them together, keeping them upright though their weary, bruised limbs longed for collapse.

She was wrong—so wrong—about so many things.

In the middle of the night, the skinless ones return but not with their usual intent. This time they are indiscriminate; everyone must go. The girl locks her arms around the sleeping child and lets herself be herded out of the cell. She hears the cries of protest from the men in an adjacent cell but knows no brave warriors will save her now. The girl tucks the child's head beneath her chin and tries to walk bravely towards her fate. The skinless ones roughly shove the terrified women down a dark hall that leads to a narrow doorway in the castle wall. Beyond is the sea.

The girl squints against the glare of the full moon hanging low in the night sky. She wills her knees not to collapse every time another captive disappears through the door with a splash. When it is her turn, she totters on the threshold and takes her last look at the world of the living. Moonlight glints off the gently rolling waves and out in the distance, a massive wooden house is magically perched upon the sea. The girl's mouth falls open in awe and then she feels rough hands hauling her downward. She drops into waist-deep water with a loud splash and is immediately bundled into a dugout canoe. Moments later, the rowers take hold of the oars and pull the canoe packed with trembling captives out to sea. Their muscular black arms gleam blue in the moonlight.

The girl has never seen water so dark and still and vast. The child's heartbeat slows and the girl dares to let herself hope. Perhaps they will be servants in the great house upon the sea. Perhaps they have left the worst of their suffering behind them.

Soon the canoe reaches the wooden house. A rope ladder dangles from above but she cannot climb it with the child in her arms. The girl tries to wake her, to shift the small body onto her back, but a cacophony of angry voices erupts from above. The rowers curse her in a language she cannot understand. Then the one closest to her simply peels the child away from her body and flings her into the sea like a small fish not worth eating.

Screaming with rage, the girl tries to plunge after the child but a fist smashes into her face and she is tossed over a rower's broad shoulder. As he pulls them up the rope ladder the girl, dazed, tries to focus her eyes on the surface of the water below. Surely someone will take pity on the child and pluck her from the sea. Surely her cries for help will pierce one other heart...

When the girl comes to, only one eye will open. There is little to see and too much to feel. Her arms are empty. Her hands and feet are shackled. Chains rattle against the wooden shelves upon which dozens of bodies writhe in terror. In the desolate blackness of the pit the girl realizes what a fool she was to hope. The worst of her suffering is not behind her—it is yet to come.

There is no time in the pit. No day or night, no earth or sky. Only moans of agony and the stench of despair as bodies empty of every fluid flesh can produce. In the cell, there had been a bucket that filled too quickly and spilled too often, but at least the women had had some way to relieve themselves. In the pit, even this dignity is denied. Skinless men appear like grimacing ghouls, their faces covered with cloths that cannot conceal their disgust. The slop they hastily and haphazardly ladle into hungry hands enters the mouth but exits almost as quickly as the pit relentlessly tosses bodies to and fro.

The girl yearns for death. The skinless ones unshackle and carry out the captives who have already expired or won't last long. The girl doesn't know where they are taken but she envies their fate. She longs to close her eyes and never open them again in the pit.

When the skinless ones return with the bucket of mush, the girl withdraws her hands as those around her clamor for their share. She closes her eyes, ignores her howling belly, and tries to imagine the child she promised to protect sleeping peacefully beneath the sea. She failed her, but at least the child did not live to witness this unending horror. Clinging to that small comfort, the girl drifts into a fitful sleep.

She wakes to a curious silence. For once there are no groans or mumbled prayers coming from her fellow captives. The wooden boards on which they lie have stopped creaking because the nauseating rocking motion in the pit has been replaced by a soothing stillness. Though food is a distant memory, the girl tastes salt upon her lips. She opens her eyes and nearly screams from shock. Inches from her own face, wrapped in a pristine indigo wrapper, is the child she cradled in her arms! The same child she left to drown.

Distrustful of her senses, the girl manages to whisper just one word. "How?"

Perched on the edge of the wooden shelf, the child beams at her and leans in to plant another salty kiss on her lips. Then, to the girl's amazement, the child opens her mouth and speaks for the first time—in her own tongue!

"I went home," she explains. "But I came back to be with you. I know how much you've missed me."

The girl nods and feels hot tears spill from her eyes. She doesn't have enough room to sit up on the platform, and the strangely still, silent bodies chained on either side of her make it difficult to move. Nonetheless the girl blinks and manages to raise her shackled hands so she can touch the child's face. "You are real? But I saw you—you sank beneath the waves…"

The child simply smiles and holds her cupped palms up to the girl's face. "Eat this."

The girl hungrily eyes the fragrant offering of boiled yam but turns her face away. "No—you must eat it to stay strong."

The child laughs and gently pries the girl's lips apart. She patiently inserts mouthfuls of food and says, "I do not need it. You do."

Unlike the bland mush from the skinless ones, the food from the child's fingers is seasoned with salt and the girl swallows the entire meal without gagging. She cannot remember the last time she felt not just full but satisfied, and the child's simple generosity brings fresh tears to her eyes. "Tell me your name so I can thank you properly."

"Call me Eja-keke," the child replies before hopping off the shelf to stand in the aisle running between the stacked captives.

The girl cranes her neck and tries to shift her body on the cramped shelf. She cannot bear to lose sight of the child again. "My name is—"

The child clamps her hand over the girl's mouth and holds it there for several seconds. Then she says, "There isn't much time. You must prepare. I will help you."

"Prepare—for what?" the girl asks anxiously but the child gives no reply.

"They left you unchained," the girl remarks. "You should leave this place. Go, hide—save yourself!"

"You are myself," Eja-keke says in a solemn voice that silences the girl. Then the child stoops to scoop up handfuls of the foul human waste pooled on the floor of the pit.

"Be still," the child commands.

The girl forces herself to obey, cringing as Eja-keke smears filth all over her face, neck, and arms. Eja-keke cannot reach her legs but the girl assures her they are just as soiled.

"This will protect you," says the child. "I promise. Now I must go."

The girl presses her hands to her chest to keep them from reaching out for the child. She can endure the miseries of the pit, but the thought of losing Eja-keke again is more than the girl can bear.

"Don't be afraid," the child calls over her shoulder before scampering down the aisle and disappearing in the darkness.

The silence and stillness Eja-keke brought to the pit suddenly dissipates. A lurching movement causes a captive on the shelf above the girl to groan before retching miserably. His vomit drips through the wooden planks onto the girl. She has no time to react because the captives on her shelf are being moved. The skinless ones return, barking orders in their ugly language. They haul the female captives off the shelf and force them to climb stairs at the far end of the pit.

Blinded by the sunlight, the women shield their eyes and huddle together. Several skinless ones snatch at their wrists and ankles, unlocking the cuffs that have rubbed their flesh raw.

Before long there is a pool of iron at their feet. They are unshackled but still not free. The girl shivers and takes a moment to look around. The sea stretches as far as her eyes can see. Sheets of white cloth attached to tall poles catch the gusts of wind that blow over the water. The wooden boards they stand upon are solid but the girl still struggles to stand upright. Finally she understands: the great wooden house does not just sit upon the sea—it moves.

A group of male captives, still shackled, is being forced to move in a circle not far from the women. Strange wheezing music comes from a skinless man holding a small box to his thin lips. Another one cracks a whip in the air, letting its stinging tail fall on the bare backs of those too weak—or too proud—to dance. The girl watches the men and sees defeat in the way most hang their heads, too ashamed to meet her gaze. Then her eyes lock on a familiar face and the girl's heart leaps. Could it be? It is! Akinde, eldest son of the chief and brother of the boy to whom she had been promised. The lash falls most often upon his broad shoulders for he is a warrior still. The pit has not crushed his defiant spirit.

Akinde's eyes meet hers for just an instant and the girl feels her face burn with shame beneath the filth Eja-keke has smeared all over her. Because of her stinking state, even the other female captives keep their distance now that the chains that bound them together have been removed. When the skinless ones suddenly toss buckets of cold salt water at the terrified women, screams fill the air. Because she stands alone, only a few drops splash against the girl's soiled skin but she winces just the same as salt licks at the open sores and cuts on her limbs. Then, without warning, the skinless men pounce upon them, each claiming a captive to devour.

The panic of the female captives drives iron into the spines of some of the men. Most are strangers but this new assault by the skinless ones stirs their warrior instincts. The wheezy music ends abruptly as Akinde and two other men break out of their tight circle and try to reach the women, dragging along several unwilling accomplices. For a moment there is total chaos: the skinless ones abandon the female captives and launch themselves at the charging men. Fists fly and the whip lashes the male captives with fury as they voice their outrage in a dozen different tongues. Akinde's words are the only ones the girl can comprehend and for a moment she forgets her fear as pride fills her soul.

"We are not beasts to be herded and whipped! We are

men—so be men! Be men!"

Akinde takes the chain that binds him and wraps it around the neck of one of the skinless men. The ghoul sputters as his face turns red. The girl watches, breathless, hopeful, and proud. Then a skinless one runs up behind Akinde and before she can call out a warning, there is a loud boom. A cloud of smoke rises from a strange stick in the skinless one's hand and Akinde's grip on the choking chain loosens as he drops to his knees.

The girl covers her face and turns away, unable to witness his death. She hears the continued crack of the whip and more shouting as the male captives are forced back into the pit. Then the skinless ones turn their attention back to the women. There is no one to help them now. The girl wrenches her arm free from the grip of a red-faced man whose skin is peeling. He pulls her close but then takes one whiff of her and hollers in disgust. The sight of his blackened teeth makes the girl recoil as well, and for a moment she finds herself unmolested. Other ghouls approach but just as quickly withdraw from her stench. She watches helplessly as the women are mauled by the skinless ones. Across the deck, two others toss Akinde's lifeless body into the sea before splashing a bucket of seawater on the deck to rinse away his blood.

"Eja-keke," the girl whispers. "Help me!"

But the child is nowhere to be seen. The girl tells herself it's good that Eja-keke has found somewhere to hide but she yearns for the child's company just the same. She creeps toward the railing over which Akinde's body was thrown. Beneath the white-capped waves the girl sees a mass, a black shadow almost as large as the boat itself. Deep underwater, in the center of the mass, is a pale light—as if the moon had fallen into the sea. Before she can take a closer look, a hand grasps her shoulder and pulls her back from the railing.

"You are a clever one," he says in a voice tinged with admiration. "Stinking—but clever."

The girl feels her mouth fall open when she turns to confront a young man with skin just a few shades lighter than her own. He is taller than her but, she suspects, only a few years older. His dark eyes don't leer at her the way the others' do and though he is dressed like the skinless ones, he speaks her tongue! For several seconds he merely studies her. She blushes but her stench seems to attract rather than repel him.

He draws closer and says, "Come," gesturing to a bucket a few feet away. "Let's clean you up a little."

When the girl refuses to move, he brings the bucket closer

and takes a blue cloth from his pocket. He dips it in the water and tries to wipe the grime off her face. When she turns her face away, he tightens his grip on her shoulder and holds her close.

"Be still," he says softly. "I won't hurt you."

The girl measures his words against the pressure of his fingers on her flesh. She looks at the women around her struggling unsuccessfully to keep the skinless ones from violating their bodies. The ghouls groan as they grope, slapping women who dare to resist their will. Trembling, the girl decides she must submit—for now.

"Are the skinless ones going to eat us?" she asks.

His lips fight the tug of a smile. "They are not skinless—their skin is just a different color than ours. And they are not going to eat you. They will sell you once we cross the sea."

The idea of being sold again gives her the courage to look him in the eye. "You speak my language—how?"

"I learned from my mother," he says as his hand slides from her shoulder to the curve of her neck. "Just as you learned from yours." He presses his thumb into the hollow at the base of her throat. "My father was captain of a ship much like this one. I speak his tongue, too. He called me Luke but you can call me Olu."

The girl hugs herself, hoping her crossed arms will stop her from shaking and prevent his hand from sliding downward. "They are savage beasts," she says quietly, lowering her eyes so he won't see her rage.

"They are sailors who have been at sea a long time. The captain allows them certain…liberties," he explains, taking her chin in his hand so she is forced to look at him. "Like bathing the female slaves."

The girl yanks her chin free. "Bathing?" She wants to spit in his face for telling such a lie. Instead she hisses, "We will never be clean again. Those men have no honor."

Olu turns her around and wrings his wet cloth so that water runs down her bare back. She feels his breath on her neck as he speaks. "You will fetch a high price. The beautiful ones always do."

The girl makes a choking sound as she tries to swallow her contempt. "Then beauty is a curse," she says sullenly.

"Yours cannot be hidden," Olu says, letting his lips brush her ear. "Not from me."

The girl feels his body pressing against her. With his hand on her waist he whispers, "I can help you—if you do as I say."

Tears fill her eyes but the girl blinks them away and reaches for the railing. The wavering light in the heart of the shadow beneath the sea seems to summon her, and she finds herself leaning forward.

Olu pulls her back from the railing. He points to several white-bellied, black-eyed beasts that roll with the waves and jostle one another in an effort to get close to the ship. Their silver fins slice through the water like blades. "Those are sharks," he says. "They follow the ship, waiting to be fed. Your friend made a good meal but they want more. They always want more."

The girl tenses but presses her lips together to stop her words from betraying her. How could he know about Akinde?

Olu seems to read her mind. "You knew him—I could tell. But he's gone now. Only I can protect you."

"And what is your price?" the girl asks over her shoulder, hoping he sees the curl of her lip.

Before Olu can answer, chaos explodes once more. A woman roars like a warrior, giving voice to the outrage of all the female captives under assault. All eyes turn toward the sailor struggling with a woman in the middle of the deck. He is trying to force his hand between her legs but the woman refuses to comply. She claws at his arms as they pry her thighs apart and then rams her fist into his groin. The sailor curses and staggers back from the woman, revealing her swollen belly. She is with child! And she is not done. The woman steps forward and grasps the ghoul's stringy hair in her hands. The girl feels her heart stop as the woman bares her teeth to the sun. Then she takes the sailor's ear between her teeth and tears with all her might.

The skinless man hollers and falls to the deck moaning in agony and clutching his head. For a brief moment the woman stands above him, triumphant. She spits his flesh out and wipes the blood from her mouth with the back of her hand. Then— before another sailor can seize her—she dashes past the girl and flings herself overboard!

Everyone gasps and rushes toward the railing. The sharks trailing the ship waste no time tearing the woman to pieces. She utters a single cry before disappearing beneath the bloody waves.

When the girl turns away from the horrific scene, her eyes land on Eja-keke. With her blue wrapper flapping in the breeze, the child claps gleefully and dances across the deck like a crazed bird. The girl tries to reach the child, to caution her against such a display. But Olu grabs the girl's arm to keep her close. A man on the ship's upper deck starts barking at the sailors. Eja-keke stops dancing, looks from the girl to Olu, and then vanishes in the crush of bodies as the sailors reluctantly follow their captain's orders. Shackles are fastened on wrists and ankles once more, and the long chain is threaded through the iron loops on each captive's cuffs.

"Next time I'll bring you a gift," Olu whispers in the girl's ear before the women are forced below deck once more.

Hours after their ordeal, women continue to weep in the blackness of the pit. The girl lies on the wooden shelf, her palm pressed into the back of the sobbing captive beside her. The women comfort one another as best they can and with what they have: silent sympathy.

Late that night the child returns with another portion of food. Once again, the sea grows calm with her arrival and without the nauseating rocking of the ship, the girl is able to eat comfortably. Eja-keke stands in the aisle, tapping out an upbeat rhythm on the edge of the platform with her little fingers.

The girl is grateful for the extra food but finds the child's buoyant mood irritating. "Why are you so happy?" she asks finally.

"Sister is free," Eja-keke says with a grin.

The girl shudders as she recalls the woman's shocking suicide. "No, she isn't—she's dead. Didn't you see all that blood in the water?"

The child's smile only widens. "Baby, too."

Eja-keke stops tapping, grips the edge of the shelf, and pulls herself up on her tips of her toes. "You could be free," she whispers in the girl's ear.

The girl stops eating and stares at the child. She imagines her own flesh being shredded by the sharp teeth of the white-bellied beasts. She sees her ravaged carcass forever sinking but never settling, never finding peace. Slowly the girl shakes her head. "The sea will not be my grave," she says quietly.

The child merely shrugs and lets go of the wooden platform. She stoops to lift the head of a young man whose skin is covered in oozing red sores. The child leans in and sniffs the corpse before letting its head fall back on the bottom shelf with a thud. "You would rather die here?" Eja-keke asks.

The girl shudders and makes no reply.

Eja-keke pulls herself up on her toes once more. She strokes the girl's matted hair and plants a kiss on the cheek Olu wiped clean with his cloth. "Next time, be nicer to him," the child advises. "Make him tell you what he knows."

"Him? Who are you talking about?" the girl asks, embarrassed to know that Eja-keke saw her talking to Olu.

"Your new friend," Eja-keke says with a smirk.

"He's not my friend," the girl snaps peevishly, turning her face away.

Eja-keke's voice loses its teasing tone. "No—he's not. But he could be a tool. Use him. Learn all you can."

The child waits to see the girl nod and then skips away down the aisle, humming to herself.

The next day, only the male captives are taken above deck. The girl strains to hear the wheezy music to which the men will be forced to dance. Next to her, a woman holds her head in her hands and starts to wail softly as clumps of hair come away from her scalp. Lying on the shelf in their collective filth, the girl thinks to herself, *We are hideous.* The darkness of the pit hides her shame, but the thought of going back up on deck makes the girl's face burn. She closes her eyes and tries to picture the light she glimpsed shining deep beneath the waves, but instead Olu's admiring eyes float in her mind.

When the female captives are unshackled the next day, the girl has to fight off two other sailors before Olu manages to claim her as his own. He pulls her away from the other victims, though privacy is impossible on the crowded, sunlit deck. Above them, the captain strides across the upper deck, ensuring his men don't disrobe. Olu explains that any contact with the female captives is allowed under that one condition.

"I have something for you," Olu says with a smile.

The girl looks down at the waxy lump in his palm. Her lack of reaction forces Olu to explain. "It's soap," he says, dropping it into a nearby bucket of water. He pulls the blue cloth from his pocket and rubs the lump over it until the bucket fills with white suds.

The girl suddenly wishes she were back in the pit, safely shackled to a dozen nameless, stinking bodies. "I can wash myself," she says but Olu insists on helping her. When he puts his soapy cloth on her breast, she angrily swats his hand away only to have Olu wrap his other hand around her neck.

"You are a slave," he reminds the girl, giving her throat an uncomfortable squeeze. "You cannot act as if you are still free. Now—let me help you."

The girl lowers her eyes and nods to show that she

understands. As Olu's hands travel over her body, she remembers Eja-keke's directive: *learn all you can.*

She cannot stop her body from trembling but the girl tries to keep her voice steady. "You said before that we are to be sold," she reminds him.

Olu nods and wipes the soapy cloth over her face, carefully avoiding her eyes. "Slaves are very valuable—especially those that can labor long hours in the hot sun. You will work with many others on a big farm."

The girl spits out the soapy water that has seeped into her mouth and then sucks her teeth at the laziness of the skinless ones. "Why do they not grow their crops themselves like we do?"

Olu scoops water out of the bucket with his hands and splashes it over her grimy body before applying his cloth. "Their farms are too large and the work is too hard. One day I will have my own farm—and my own slaves to help me."

He looks at her meaningfully but the girl avoids his eyes. She wishes Eja-keke were here to direct the conversation. Though just a child, she would know the best questions to ask. "What do they grow on these farms?" the girl asks finally.

"Different things: tobacco, cotton, rice. Also sugarcane," he

MOTHER OF THE SEA

replies. When he sees her confusion he adds, "Tall green stalks that you cut with a machete."

"Machete?"

"A tool with a long, sharp blade," he explains.

Any blade that can cut stalks can cut men down, too. The girl looks away, careful to compose her face so that he will misread her cunning for curiosity.

"Where will we get these tools?" she asks, looking straight into Olu's eyes to assure him of her innocence.

His hands linger on her bare hips. The desire in Olu's eyes makes the girl wish she were as emaciated as some of the other captives. She silently vows to refuse the next offering of food Eja-keke brings her.

Olu's breath is coming fast. He clears his throat and tries to reassure her. "The overseer will give you the tools you need."

"And where do they get such tools?" the girl asks, taking the cloth from Olu's hand and rubbing it along her neck.

He pulls her closer. "We sell them in the market. This ship carries supplies as well as slaves—everything a plantation owner needs."

The soapy water makes it easy for his hands to slip over her skin quickly, but Olu's palms move slowly despite the suds. The girl takes a step back even though she knows he can simply reach out and pull her close again—or pass her to another sailor. The only escape is to throw herself into the sea where the sharks await.

She turns her back to Olu and looks up to find Eja-keke peering at her through the rails of the upper deck. The captain seems oblivious to the child even though she is crouching just a few feet away. The girl feels certain that Eja-keke is charmed. How else could such an innocent child survive in such an evil place? The girl decides she will ask Eja-keke to teach her how to make herself invisible.

She cringes as Olu presses his lips to the back of her neck. He is not a brute like the others. Olu is gentle compared to them, but he still has no right to touch her this way. The girl remembers what Eja-keke told her in the pit: *He is not your friend.* Much as she craves tenderness and protection, she knows Olu is merely using her, taking advantage of her powerlessness. The girl searches for words to distract him but cannot think of a way to make him her tool.

"Please stop," she says softly, hating herself for sounding so weak. The girl remembers the woman, big with child, who tore the ear off her assailant. Why can't she find such courage within herself?

Olu is mumbling words she cannot understand. When the captain barks more foreign words, Olu spins her around and covers her lips with his own. The girl struggles to breathe but cannot push him away. She finally manages to turn her face aside and pleads, "Please don't…"

Olu holds her close but stops kissing her. With his mouth pressed to her ear he says, "I've been saving for a long time so I can buy a piece of land. If I had enough money," he says wistfully, "I would buy you instead."

His grip finally loosens and the girl staggers back as if she has been punched in the belly. She quickly masks her rage and lines up with the other captives to be shackled once more.

When the pit grows still in the middle of the night, Eja-keke returns. In her hands she holds a small ivory comb instead of food. She climbs up onto the middle shelf and patiently begins to untangle the girl's hair.

Distant memories of her mother massaging oil into her scalp bring bitter tears to the girl's eyes. She can no longer count the priceless things she has lost. Eja-keke lets her weep softly, occasionally pausing to wipe the girl's face with the edge of her cloth wrapper.

"How do you do it?" the girl asks Eja-keke in a wavering voice. "How do you make yourself invisible to them?"

"Hush," the child says with a gentle caress. "It will be over soon."

The girl hopes Eja-keke is telling the truth but her heavy heart remains unconvinced. "Olu says we'll all be sold when the ship crosses the sea," she tells Eja-keke.

The child laughs as she twines strands of the girl's hair into tiny braids. "That won't happen," she says, proudly patting her handiwork.

"How do you know?" the girl asks.

Eja-keke pauses, seeming to weigh the risks of revealing a secret. Finally she says firmly, "No one will be sold—I promise."

For a long while they sit together in companionable silence. The girl grows drowsy and lets Eja-keke turn her head as needed until her scalp is covered in neat braids.

"He will be yours to command," the child declares.

The girl's eyes flash open and she fights the sudden urge to rip her hair from her head. "Make me disappear—please," she begs.

Eja-keke shakes her head. "It will be over soon. I found them," the child confides. "I know where they are."

Panic grips the girl. "They?" she asks anxiously. "Stay away from the sailors! They'll kill you or—or worse."

Eja-keke puts a hand to her mouth to smother a giggle. Then she rests a single finger on the girl's lips. The child winks and whispers, "Not them—the machetes!"

The girl studies Eja-keke's face and marvels at her mask of perfect innocence. Yet something in the child's glittering black eyes makes her uneasy.

Eja-keke's smile starts to fade. "Say something," she demands petulantly.

The girl settles on her back and stares up at the shelf above to avoid looking at the child. "What do you want me to say?" she asks quietly.

"You told me you wanted to be free," Eja-keke reminds her.

"How can a farm tool set me free?"

Eja-keke leans close and hisses in her ear. "One cannot. But dozens of blades in dozens of hands will bring death to the skinless ones!" Eja-keke pauses and studies the girl. "Isn't that what you want—to make them pay for all they've done?"

The girl sighs and closes her eyes. She sees brave Akinde falling to his knees, blood pooling around him on the deck. "We are not warriors," she says flatly. "We are slaves—starved, beaten, and chained like beasts in this pit. Most of the men are already defeated. They will not fight for us."

Eja-keke sucks her teeth in disgust. "Do *you* not have hands? A woman can wield a weapon as easily as any man. My mother is a great warrior," she says with pride.

"Your mother isn't here," the girl replies testily.

"Yes, she is," Eja-keke says quietly.

Something in the child's voice makes the girl look at her once more. Eja-keke flashes her a mischievous smile before hopping off the shelf and running away.

For several days the captives are not allowed above deck. Storms batter the ship, leaving the crew no time to tend to those chained below. Eja-keke stays away as well, and the girl suffers terrifying dreams that leave her feverish and delirious. When she finally wakes, the sea is calm once more. The hatch is opened and sailors descend with their bucket of mush. The women are fed while the male captives are taken above deck for exercise. Then, to her surprise, the women are taken out of the pit as well. They are doused with buckets of seawater but their shackles and chains are not removed. Expecting the usual scramble that precedes their assault, the female captives instead are herded to one side of the deck and told to sit. Two sailors go back into the pit with buckets and mops. Others climb the wooden poles to take down the white sail that has been shredded by the fierce winds.

The girl kneels upon the deck and surveys the strange scene. The male captives, looking weak and weary, are seated on the other side of the ship. Three sailors stand over them, each holding the strange stick that killed Akinde. The girl searches for Eja-keke's bright blue wrapper but cannot spot the child and feels a sense of relief. She shifts closer to the ship's railing and peers into the sea. The black shadow that has followed the ship across the sea is also nowhere to be found, but in its place are more sharks than she can count.

The girl's heart thuds loudly in her chest. Something isn't right. Something is about to happen.

She is so preoccupied that she doesn't see Olu until he towers above her. Without a word, he hands her his blue kerchief. The girl takes it and finds a lump of soap wrapped inside the cloth.

"I'll bring water so you can bathe," Olu says. His fingers lightly stroke her braided hair. She shudders when she sees the coiled leather whip in his other hand.

The girl wants to hurl Olu's gift into the sea but instead she conceals it as best she can in her shackled hands. She dares not meet the eyes of the other female captives. What must they think of her? The girl keeps her eyes lowered and hopes they understand.

She decides she will share the soap with the other women but when Olu returns, he sets the bucket down at his feet. When the girl tries to pull it closer, Olu orders her to leave it be.

"You can bathe here next to me," he says.

The girl kneels next to the bucket and drops the bundle he gave her into the water.

"Stand up," he tells her. "I want to see you."

The sun blazes overhead but it is shame that makes her face burn. The girl tugs at the chain binding her to the other women. "I cannot stand," she reminds him, "unless we all stand."

Annoyed, Olu scans the deck and mutters something in his father's tongue. "I'll get the key," he says to the girl before striding off once more.

The girl takes this opportunity to move the bucket closer to the other women. She rubs the soap into a lather and offers the cloth to the captive next to her. That woman turns her face away but other eager hands reach out for the cloth. The captives manage to form a sort of circle around the bucket and the cloth is passed back and forth. There is only enough water for them to wash their faces but the women seem grateful for even this small kindness.

As they bathe, the girl keeps one eye on Olu. He goes from sailor to sailor but seems no closer to finding what he desires. Suddenly frantic yelling comes from below deck. Everyone freezes and then gasps in horror as a sailor drags himself out of the pit. He clutches his throat but blood still manages to spurt through his fingers.

Attention is focused on the dying man so no one notices the small child who slips out of the pit a moment later. Eja-keke scurries over to the girl and the women close around her instinctively. Her blue wrapper is soaked in blood but the child is bursting with joy.

The girl grabs Eja-keke by the shoulders and inspects her. "Are you hurt? What happened to you?"

The child wriggles free and gazes upon her bloody wrapper with pride. She looks up at the girl and whispers, "Machete!"

Before the girl can think how to respond, Eja-keke grabs her wrist. Her little fingers are sticky with blood but she easily inserts the key that unlocks the iron cuff. She then hands the key to the girl and says, "You do that one."

Eja-keke watches with satisfaction as the girl inserts the key and unlocks the cuff on her other wrist. "Now do your feet," she says.

The girl obeys and steps out of the cuffs that bound her ankles together. When she tries to free the captive next to her, the woman yanks her shackled hands away and turns her back on the girl. She is more selective after that. She has no time for those who are ruled by fear. If she can free enough who still have the will to fight, perhaps she can find the machetes and put them in the right hands.

The girl holds out the key and looks into the faces of her fellow captives. A woman with delicate crescents carved along her cheekbones pushes forward to claim the key. The girl surrenders it with a silent nod and leaves the rest of the captives to free themselves. With no common language, the women work wordlessly and wisely remain huddled together to give the illusion that they are still chained.

They are unguarded—for now. The girl realizes with relief

that Olu has forgotten her. Sailors are running up and down the stairs that lead into the pit, shouting words the girl cannot understand. Two men emerge carrying a second body, also covered in blood. The sailors set it down on the deck as gently as they can but the nearly severed head lolls unnaturally. One sailor turns aside and vomits. The others fume and gesticulate, with most fingers pointing in the direction of the male captives. But they have been on deck the whole time.

The girl recalls Eja-keke's indignant words: *A woman can wield a weapon as easily as any man*. These men do not know what she is capable of and that is perhaps her only advantage. But she knows the sailors' rage will soon fall upon the child. The girl can't think of anywhere on the ship to hide Eja-keke, but vows that this time—*this time*—she will give her life before letting anyone harm a hair on her head.

But Eja-keke does not seek her protection. Panic stabs the girl's heart when she finds that the headstrong child has vanished. The girl looks past the knot of anxious sailors in the middle of the deck and spots the child crouching next to a male captive on the far side of the ship. The sullen look on his face shifts almost imperceptibly when she presses something into his hand. Another key? The girl feels a pang of guilt. She should have paid attention the last time Eja-keke came to her at night. The child had been eager to share her plan but the girl had pushed her away. Now Eja-keke is acting alone.

The girl watches as Eja-keke calmly steps past the armed sailors who are guarding the male captives. She wedges her small body between those hovering above the dying man like vultures. Eja-keke pauses to admire the nearly headless corpse before standing directly in front of the sailor whose throat she slit. He gasps at the sight of her and uses the last of his strength to point an accusing finger at the child.

His fellow sailors reel in shock. For the first time, Eja-keke sheds whatever magic has made her invisible to them. She laughs as her second victim expires and is immediately grabbed by a stout sailor with shaggy, copper-colored hair.

"No!" the girl screams. She plunges into their midst and tries to reach Eja-keke. "Don't touch her! She does not belong to you!"

The girl knows they cannot understand her words, but there is no mistaking her tone. She senses the other captives stirring on the deck. If she leads, will they follow? Together they can save Eja-keke—maybe even save themselves. The girl searches for a gesture that will rally the captives but her outburst only earns her a backhanded blow from the captain. She staggers back, dazed, but regains her footing, supported by the hands of the female captives. Their hands push her forward once more and then Olu is at her side.

Only I can protect you.

Grateful, the girl smiles at him but Olu's hand squeezes the air out of her throat as he lifts her almost off the ground.

"Be quiet!" he hisses with a furious glare. "Do you want to be next?"

The girl cannot respond so Olu throws her to the deck and cracks his whip over the heads of the female captives. They shrink from the lash but form a protective shell and do what they can to help the girl as she sputters for air.

He's not my friend.

After a moment, the girl recovers enough to once more fix her gaze on Eja-keke. The child is smiling despite the sailor's rough grip on her arms.

Use him. Learn all you can.

The girl brushes away the pleading hands of the other women and gets to her feet. Olu is meant to be guarding them but his attention is drawn to the circle of sailors arguing in the middle of the deck. The girl approaches silently and lightly presses her fingertips into Olu's back. He glances over his shoulder and, seeing her head bowed in submission, allows her to remain.

The girl waits a few moments before daring to speak. She doesn't have much time but cannot let Olu hear the urgency behind her words. "What are they saying?" she asks quietly.

He grunts without looking at her. "They think she's a witch," Olu says.

A cloud covers the sun. The girl blinks as her eyes adjust to the new light. Is Eja-keke's bizarre smile actually a grimace? Her arms are being twisted behind her back and look as if they might snap in the sailor's cruel hands.

The girl forces a light laugh. "You don't believe that—she's just a child."

"A child who killed two men," Olu says. He jerks his body to shake her fingers off his back. "Sit down."

The girl reluctantly obeys but the argument escalates, with two sailors nearly coming to blows. One with sand-colored hair points to the dead men and then at Eja-keke. He draws his hand across his threat, mimicking the slicing motion of a blade.

The cloud covering the sun merges with others, casting a shadow over the ship. On her knees, the girl inches closer to

Olu once more and cautiously wraps her arm around his calf. She leans against him hoping the gesture will convince him of her loyalty.

When Olu doesn't push her away, she dares to ask another question. "They're going to kill her?"

"Yes," he replies without emotion. The girl bows her head and hopes he will go on. She feels the light patter of rain on her bare skin.

Olu's absently strokes her hair as he translates the debate unfolding on deck. "Some want to behead her," he explains. "Others just want to throw her overboard. But the first mate says he saw her thrown into the sea once before—back at the coast. He says she cannot be killed that way. Only fire will do."

The girl bites down on her lip until she tastes blood. She has to do something. She cannot sit idly by Olu's side like a loyal pet while these fiends decide Eja-keke's fate. The girl searches the faces of the male captives until she finds the one who took the key from Eja-keke. She stares at the sullen man, willing him to look her way. After several seconds, the man turns his head and looks into the girl's eyes. He seems to read the desperation there because he nods once before turning his gaze back to the bickering sailors.

The girl looks over her shoulder at the female captives cowering behind her. She scans the group until she finds the woman with the crescent markings on her face. The girl wants to say, "Sister, help me," but she has no words this woman will understand. Instead the girl keeps her unblinking gaze trained on the woman's face until she, too, turns and reads the message in her eyes. *We must act—now.*

The barking stops suddenly and the sailors scatter as they attend to different tasks. Four of them carry away the bodies of the dead men. Another brings a wooden chair out of the captain's cabin. Still holding her by the arms, the copper-haired sailor slams Eja-keke onto the chair while another man binds her with rope. Through it all Eja-keke smiles and patiently tolerates their rough treatment. When a sailor leans in and spits in her face, she laughs.

The wind picks up suddenly and the ship rolls in the swelling waves. The girl tightens her grip on Olu's leg. "Are they really going to burn her?" she asks.

He nods. "It will be quick," he assures her. "They're using whale oil. The smoke will choke her before she can feel the flames."

The girl can tell he is lying. She looks up at Olu and

wonders if this is how he imagined their future together—the whip in his hand and her curled at his feet like a dog. She removes her arm and shifts away from him. The clouds overhead darken ominously as rain begins to fall.

The captain is standing next to Eja-keke. He makes a pronouncement that only the sailors can understand and then steps aside to make room for another man who holds a torch. The wind whips fiercely, almost extinguishing the flame. The sailor staggers back as the ship lurches in the choppy sea. Then he leans into the wind and touches the wavering torch to Eja-keke's oil- and blood-soaked wrapper.

The girl stands and puts her hand on Olu's arm. When he jerks his arm away, she grabs him again—harder this time. He turns, ready to strike her with the raised whip. That is when Olu realizes that she is not chained. The girl balls her fingers and drives her fist into his groin. Stunned, Olu goes down with a wordless gasp and in that moment, the crescent woman snatches the whip from his hand and lunges at the sailor holding the torch. She loops the leather around his neck and pulls back with all her might. The torch falls to the deck as rain pours down with sudden, terrifying intensity.

Eja-keke—seconds from an agonizing death—squeals with

glee as the raindrops douse the fire intended to destroy her. The male captives seize the moment and spring upon the sailors, using their chains to exact revenge. They soon learn that the guns can only be fired once and when one captive falls, another charges forward to take his place. Others, too frightened to fight, cower against the railing of the ship. Massive waves crash over the deck, washing sailors and captives alike into the sea.

As the sky blackens above, the girl scrambles through the warring bodies and torrential rain to reach Eja-keke. Her fingers fumble with the knots and she looks around for something sharp to cut the rope.

"The machetes," cries the girl. "Where are they?"

But Eja-keke refuses to answer. Thunder booms and the sea begins to spiral upwards into the sky. The girl gapes in awe at the pillars of water. She throws her body over the child, fearful she will be swept into the sea. But Eja-keke is fearless as ever, singing as the storm rages around her. *Yeye Omo Eja! Yeye Omo Eja! My mother is here! Go now—we are free! My mother is here!*

"I won't leave you," the girl shouts, hoping the weight of her body will be enough to anchor Eja-keke to the deck. This time she will not let go, even if they are swept into the sea.

Suddenly, above the roar of thunder, the girl hears another, more ominous sound. She feels the deck shudder and then screams as the ship begins to break apart. The tall poles that once held its sails crack and fall, crushing those below. Then the ship snaps in half and everything that was on or near the surface of the sea lifts up into the air. Shards of wood, iron shackles, and human beings—both dead and alive—swirl in a dizzying cone that seems to race across the water. When she loses sight of Eja-keke, the girl surrenders to the storm, knowing the end is near. Despite the deafening howl of the wind, she can still hear Eja-keke's joyous song: *Yeye Omo Eja! Yeye Omo Eja! My mother is here! We are free!*

When the girl wakes, the black sky no longer rumbles with thunder. She blinks to bring her eyes into focus and sees a night sky filled with stars. The silence around her is so complete that the girl wonders if she has lost the ability to hear. Then, slowly, sound returns. The girl hears the soft splash of waves lapping against the shore. She finds she cannot move her battered limbs but with effort, the girl manages to turn her head. She sees a beach strewn with broken bodies and the shattered remains of the ship.

The girl closes her eyes and lies on the sand with the waves licking at her feet. Her heart aches more than her bruised body. She has survived the shipwreck, but is she free? The pit is no more and the fiends who built it are gone. But what about the child she swore to protect?

The full moon accuses her. It was just as bright the first time she let Eja-keke be snatched from her arms. Groaning with pain she feels she deserves, the girl pulls herself upright. She gazes upon the calm waves, awed by their ability to conceal such peril. Despite her grief, the girl feels a newfound respect for the sea. She would make it an offering but she is utterly bereft.

Dragging herself to her feet, the girl staggers along the beach in a hopeless search for the child. Amidst the flotsam she finds several corpses still chained together, their open eyes frozen in horror. The girl stumbles on and sees up ahead a woman dragging herself from the sea. Though she is unshackled, the woman doesn't have enough strength to keep her head out of the water, and when the girl reaches her, she doesn't have enough strength to pull the woman to shore. So the girl falls to her knees in the shallow water and lifts the woman's head into her lap. She mumbles words the girl cannot understand but there is no mistaking the crescent markings on her face.

"Rest now, Sister," the girl whispers. "We are together again. We are free."

They cling to one another at the edge of the sea. Time passes and clouds gather, blotting out the moon. Lightning flashes in the distance and a strong wind begins to blow, but the girl is no longer afraid. She has survived the worst the sea can do. So she does not flinch when a giant wave rolls toward the shore and rises like a wall before her and her friend. Instead of crashing over them, the wave holds without cresting. A strange light glows within its depths and then a shadow—a Spirit— emerges from the wall of water in the form of a woman.

Aduke.

The word leaves the Spirit's lips and settles like a blessing upon the girl. She cannot remember the last time she heard her name spoken with such love.

I never left you, the Spirit says with a voice like distant thunder.

The girl nods and tears spill down her cheeks. "I know," she replies, instantly recognizing the black mass that trailed the ship across the sea. That light the girl saw gleaming beneath the waves is an enormous pearl that hangs between the Spirit's full breasts. Her dense black hair moves like a net cast over her shoulders, bursting with life dredged from the sea. Shimmering eels and brightly colored fish weave in and out of her tightly coiled locks. When she smiles, her teeth flash against her dark skin like cowries.

The Spirit stretches out her arms. Like her legs, they are covered in silver scales. *Come, my children,* she says. It is an invitation and a command.

Water swirls around the girl and her friend, making it easy for them to rise. The corpses farther down the beach stand as well and wade into the water. As their chains fall away, their eyes close upon the horrors of the past. They walk, blind and serene, into the sea.

The Spirit gathers them in a mother's loving embrace and together they begin the long walk home.

Aduke: beloved

Adun: sweetness

Akinde: a warrior has arrived

Eja-keke: little fish

Oluseyi: God has made this

Yeye-omo-eja: mother whose children are like fish (Yemoja)

I don't remember when I heard my first mermaid story. I recall the dreamy video for Sade's 1992 hit "No Ordinary Love," and know that I took my younger siblings to see Disney's *The Little Mermaid* when I was a teen. Around that same time I discovered a feminist retelling of the Arthurian legend; reading *The Mists of Avalon* changed the way I looked at fairy tales, and by the time I graduated from college, I'd become wary of literary references to mermaids as sinister female figures who lured men to their deaths. But it wasn't until I started doing research on my family's Caribbean roots in 2012 that I decided to write my own mermaid story.

When I learned of the mass suicide committed by enslaved men on board *The Prince of Orange* in 1737, I began plotting a story about a mischievous girl who lived beneath the sea but could still wreak havoc on land by mobilizing her underwater army. I haven't written that story yet, but when I was asked to contribute a piece of flash fiction for AnomalyCon 2017, I wrote a 100-word sketch based on another mass suicide at Igbo Landing, off the coast of Georgia, in 1803:

> The girl looks down and wonders which devil's hands fashioned the shackles that bind her small feet. Her people know how to work iron but she has never seen chains, collars, and manacles like these.
>
> She winces as the wind blows against the open sores on her limbs and the chafed skin around her ankles. All their wounds are sticky with blood and pus. Nothing heals or even scabs over in the pit.
>
> Now there is air and light but the land cannot hold them. She inches closer to the water, fearing yet craving the sting of salt.
>
> "Soon?"
>
> Her voice holds enough respect to earn another response from the ancient one.
>
> A nod. A hoarse whisper. *Soon.*
>
> Wet sand sucks against the soles of her restless feet. Down the line, iron links begin to ring like muffled bells.
>
> The crone smiles and nudges her forward.
>
> *Go to her. Let the spirit of the sea guide you.*
>
> The girl winces, then shivers as the waves pull her into the sea.
>
> *Soon.*
>
> Home.

I had the chance to further develop this story when I accepted a commission to write a science fiction/fantasy narrative for an eighth-grade English Language Arts curriculum. The unit included *The Hunger Games*, one of Ray Bradbury's short stories, and *City of Beasts* by Isabel Allende. I wanted my contribution to illustrate a point I raised in a 2013 article for *Bitch Media*, "Black Girls Hunger for Heroes, Too: A Black Feminist Conversation on Fantasy Fiction for Teens:"

> I haven't read the [*Hunger Games*] trilogy, but I watched the first film at home and the second one in the theater. And when it got to the part where Gale was being whipped, I could sense the tension in the [interracial] audience. And I thought to myself: "How many people in here went to see *12 Years a Slave*?" It's interesting to me that in the white imagination, the dystopian future involves white people living through the realities that people of color have lived or are living through right now!

Most US students in the eighth grade know little if anything about the Middle Passage and/or West African religions, so I pitched a story about a slave ship that is ultimately destroyed by the Ifá orisha Yemoja (known as Yemayá in the Americas). When I teach my students about the trans-Atlantic slave trade, I show them the Middle Passage scene from the film *Amistad*. The hero of that 1839 slave ship rebellion is Cinqué (or Sengbe) but for my story, I imagined an uprising led by a young woman. When I searched online for images of a Black mermaid, I was most struck by the depictions of Yemoja wielding a machete and was thrilled to find artist Christina Myrvold who, I think, perfectly captured Yemoja's dual aspects: a loving mother who protects, defends, but also disciplines her children.

I grew up in a devout Christian family full of preachers and teachers. Other religions were never discussed and I was forced to attend church so long as I lived at home. As a teenager I felt contempt for my parents' blind faith yet I also felt somewhat ashamed of my own disinterest in religion. What I loved were the stories of miracles that left true believers unscathed by fire, untouched by lions—healed, whole, and happy. As a Black feminist writer I am committed to telling stories that center and empower Black women and girls, but I am also very aware of my ignorance when it comes to African religions and cultures. Writing as an outsider means grappling with the Middle Passage or what fellow Canadian writer Dionne Brand calls "a tear in the world…a rupture in history, a rupture in the quality of being…a physical rupture, a rupture of geography." In *A Map to the Door of No Return* (2001), Brand brilliantly articulates the struggle of artists throughout the diaspora:

> Africa. It was the place we did not remember, yet it lodged itself in all the conversations of who we were. It was a visible secret. Through the BBC broadcasts we were inhabited by British consciousness. We were also inhabited by an unknown self. The African…One had the sense that some being had to be erased and some being had to be cultivated. Even our dreams were not free of this conflict. We floated on an imaginary island imagining a "Dark Continent." That "Dark Continent" was a source of denial and awkward embrace. The African self so abiding yet so fearful because it was informed by colonial images of the African as savage and not by anything we could call on our memories to conjure.

It is humbling to have to "cultivate" an understanding and appreciation of beliefs which my ancestors likely practiced organically, but it is also important to acknowledge that rupture and its lasting effects. My attempt to incorporate elements of African religions into my stories is indeed "awkward," and I apologize for any errors or inaccuracies. I'm thankful for the assistance with Yoruba names provided by Funlayo E. Wood and Dupe Oluyomi-Obasi. I am also deeply grateful for the feedback and insights provided by Dupe's mother, anthropologist Sarah Oluyomi:

> ...traditionally, in the pre-colonial era, women played significant roles in all spheres of life. This is evident in many of the religious practices, oral traditions and myths. Most of the Yoruba religious practices function as informal socialization agents that help the people learn and adopt the beliefs, values and norms that are represented in the nonmaterial Yoruba culture.

> Yemoja worship...is institutionalized in order to teach members of the Yoruba society that women are productive agents and/or political influencers who are capable of producing something/someone and who also have the ability to effect and affect a person or situation significantly. To date, for example, prior to any king been enthroned, it is customary among the Yoruba people where Yemoja is worshipped, for the traditional chiefs to consult the oracle through the Yemoja priestess. The purpose is to confirm the candidacy of the aspirant and to determine which rituals should be performed. At the same time, women are perceived as representing agents of peace and gentleness. Hence, you have Yemoja as an agent of socialization through which the image of women is formed as the powerful and productive mother, a protector of her children and a giver of life.

Most of my writing for teens focuses on Black girls' search for empowerment as they mature into young women. With *Mother of the Sea*, I tried to show parallel journeys: Aduke's forced relocation from Africa to the Americas, and her evolution from a frightened, despondent girl into a daring rebel and leader. When teens in the US look for a Black woman superhero, their options are fairly limited; I hope Yemoja can stand alongside Storm as a symbol of African female power.

In 2010 I wrote an essay, "Decolonizing the Imagination," about my goal of moving young people "beyond wands and wizards." But in order for them to embrace "Black magic," they have to recognize and release the many distortions that have led too many kids in our communities to disparage all things African. With her *Lemonade* album and recent Grammy performance, Beyoncé has introduced millions to Oshun; some dismiss her invocation of the orisha as a gimmick, but I see it as an important start to a much needed conversation and a way to strip the shame many still feel around African spiritual practices.

I am not Beyoncé. But I feel I can still play an important role as someone who works with, and writes for, children and teens. When I realized this 10,000-word story would not work for the ELA curriculum (they asked for 3,000 words), I immediately decided to self-publish it as a novelette. I hope to use *Mother of the Sea* in high school classrooms and urge you to share it with the young readers in your life. In this frightening political moment of "alternative facts," it's vital that we "teach the youth the truth." And as we teach, we learn.

Zetta Elliott
April 7, 2017
Brooklyn, NY

ABOUT THE AUTHOR

Born in Canada, Zetta Elliott moved to the US in 1994 to pursue her PhD in American Studies at NYU. Her poetry has been published in several anthologies, and her plays have been staged in New York, Chicago, and Cleveland. Her essays have appeared in *The Huffington Post*, *School Library Journal*, and *Publishers Weekly*. She is the author of over twenty books for young readers, including the award-winning picture book *Bird*. Her urban fantasy novel, *Ship of Souls*, was named a *Booklist* Top Ten Sci-fi/Fantasy Title for Youth; her latest picture book, *Melena's Jubilee*, was named one of "100 Magnificent Children's Books" by Betsy Bird. Three books published under her own imprint, Rosetta Press, have been named Best Children's Books of the Year by the Bank Street Center for Children's Literature. Rosetta Press generates culturally relevant stories that center children who have been marginalized, misrepresented, and/or rendered invisible in traditional children's literature. Elliott is an advocate for greater diversity and equity in publishing. She currently lives in Brooklyn. Learn more at www.zettaelliott.com

ABOUT THE ARTIST

Christina Myrvold is a professional freelance artist specializing in concept art, illustration, graphic design, and environment and character design. She is currently based in Middlesbrough, UK. Find prints at www.zazzle.com/christinamyrvold/products

Made in the USA
Columbia, SC
21 December 2018